A MIRACLE IN SAL.

Hope over Despair, Love over Indifference.

Introduction:

We are sometimes challenged by difficult circumstances, which can tempt us to despair. However, as we are on the point of sinking a door of hope is suddenly and unexpectedly opened to us.

We realise that all is not lost, but that we can be confident that a different outcome is possible - our future will bring blessings and not a curse.

As we open the eyes of our imagination, we can experience grace and favour, which we don't deserve, but they are offered to us.

As you read this book, you will discover twin themes of hope and grace. Hope for the oppressed and exploited - Leah, her son Andy, and their neighbours and work colleagues - and grace for those who, like Thomas, Leah's employer, is cruel in heart and a tyrant in all of his ways.

I won't spoil the story for you by telling you what happens.

You must read and enjoy!

The setting is a small town in Sal.

Although this is not explicitly mentioned, we may assume this is a town in a developing country - a country in Africa, perhaps.

You may have heard or even experienced bosses who mistreat their employees and so here comes a wealthy man called Thomas, who employs the town dwellers on his plantation, rather than sharing his resources, exploits their labour and mistreats them.

Leah, a single mother, and her nine-year old son Andy, suffer greatly because of Thomas' abusive behaviour.

Leah's suffering intensifies until she becomes very unwell and experiences a crisis.

Andy, her son, shows what it means to truly love, and devotes all of his energy to ensuring that his mother receives the help which she needs.

His desire is to see her well and happy again.

Andy's unfailing loyalty, faithfulness and perseverance reap a reward, inasmuch as he finds the joy and freedom he so earnestly desires.

His hope is not disappointed.

Leah not only experiences a profound personal transformation, but his own life - indeed, the lives of all of the town dwellers - are touched and changed too.

Belief in the reality of providence is also another powerful theme in this book.

We often assume that our lives are our own and that we can control and plan for what lies ahead. However, a truly wise person knows that the contrary is true: there is much we don't, indeed can't, control.

As we reflect on our lives, we discover that events and circumstances often work together for our good.

If we seek what is right, we find that there is one who is guiding and caring for us, who brings the right set of circumstances and people into our lives at the right time.

We may or may not recognise this Presence to be God. Nevertheless, we will find that we have been blessed in unexpected ways.

Amazingly Providence even cares for and intervenes on the behalf of those who are not good.

Thomas, who is unlikeable and seemingly irredeemable, is offered grace and joy of joys; he accepts the invitation which is given and becomes a wholly different person.

Please take the opportunity to pause and reflect on this story and to be transformed by it.

Then pass the book to someone else to read and enjoy - perhaps a family member, friend or work colleague; and they, in turn, can recommend it to the people they know.

A Town Called Sal

Chapter 1 - Thomas.

A man, whose name was Thomas, lived in a small town called Sal. His wife was widely admired as she was a beautiful woman. His two children were also beautiful.

He had enough money to meet all of his family's basic needs. Indeed, he was the richest man in the local area. His children went to good schools in the city. He was a farmer who earned his living from rearing cows, goats, sheep and pigs and selling the produce.

In recent years he had diversified the variety of animals to include chickens, turkeys and ducks.

He also owned a large plantation of banana plantain.

His farm and plantation offered employment to the people of the local area, including his immediate neighbours.

Thomas was not a friendly man. He was arrogant and unapproachable.

Sadly, his wife and children were tainted by his bad example and behaved in a similar way.

Often Thomas would boast to his workers that they couldn't survive without him. They resented his mistreatment of them, but couldn't leave, as alternative work was not available.

Some of his workers were single mothers. They worked for ten hours every day. They dug his plantation using hands and hoes. This was very tiring work. However, they still did their best and worked wholeheartedly.

Thomas and his wife did not appreciate their loyalty and commitment. Everyone who worked for them was treated harshly.

No-one was respected.

Thomas did not give his workers anything to eat or drink for the whole day, in spite of owning ample resources, from which he could have made generous provision.

To add insult to injury, Thomas and his family ate good meals in the presence of the workers. Any leftovers were given to the pigs.

The workers were not even allowed to go home at lunchtime to get something to eat. If they did go home for lunch without his consent, Thomas would give them half pay only.

So some workers started to take packed lunches to work. At lunchtime they would share it with those who could not afford to buy enough food for themselves.

On one occasion Leah, who was one of the workers, felt hungry and had a severe stomach-ache.

She was too afraid to ask her workmates for food because it was not yet lunchtime. So she decided to go to Thomas' wife for help.

She explained what her difficulty was, but Thomas` wife was not bothered at all. Looking at her from head to foot with a condescending expression, she said, "there is no free food here!"

She warned Leah that her pay would be halved if she did not return to work.

Still feeling very hungry, and lacking any other means of help, she sneaked into the pigs' house and ate some of the leftovers.

Thomas, who was standing nearby but hidden from sight, saw her eating. He was indignant.

"How could you do this, Leah?" he shouted. "You know very well how important my pigs are.

How dare you eat their food?"

"Please forgive me, sir. I was so hungry and I had no option. I promise I won't do it again," Leah pleaded.

Thomas would not listen to Leah's excuse. He quickly grabbed a big stick and hit her several times. "I don't care whether you were hungry or not," he shouted.

"Listen to me very carefully. If I ever find you eating their food again, I will teach you a lesson that you will never forget for the rest of your life.

Do you understand?"

"Yes, sir," Leah replied, while wiping tears from her face.

"As for today, I will not pay you," Thomas said. "The money I was supposed to give you will cover the food that you have just eaten."

"Please, sir," Leah pleaded. "Please don't hold onto the money that I have worked for. At least give me half of it."

Shaking his head, Thomas replied, "I swear, Leah, I will not pay you!"

Unable to stop the tears which were flowing down her face - so great was her anxiety and suffering, Leah knelt down and explained to him what she was going through.

"You know I am a single mother with many challenges. I have no food to feed my son, my only child. We are starving. Please have mercy upon me!"

Thomas, who was burning with rage, shouted, "Leah, get out of my sight!"

But Leah was so desperate she continued to plead with him. "Please, sir?
Please forgive me!"

Thomas, whose anger had now reached boiling point, slapped her. "Whether you and your son starve is none of my business," he shouted.

Chapter 2 - Threats and Kindness.

When Leah told the other workers of how she had been treated, they felt very sorry for her.

They begged Thomas to forgive her and pay her the money she had worked for, but Thomas refused to listen.

"Okay, if you all insist that I pay her, then I will cut off your pay as well!" he threatened.

"No, sir! Please don't do that to us," Jehu and the rest of the workers said together.

Thomas would not relent and did not pay Leah her money.

Melissa, who was one of her workmates, looked at Leah and said, "Leah, but why didn't you tell us that you were very hungry?

We would have helped you. We are in this together.

Next time, don't be afraid to share your problems with us. Is that okay?"

"Okay, Melissa," Leah agreed.

"Good. Now, after work, let's go together and I will give you potatoes and beans. I have some at home which we can share."

"Thank you, Melissa. Thank you very much." Leah felt very relieved.

Later that evening they went together to Melissa`s home. Melissa gave Leah enough potatoes, beans and corn flour to last for a few days.

"Oh! My goodness! What can I say, Melissa! " Leah said with a big smile.

"It's okay, Leah," Melissa said.

A few minutes later Leah said goodbye to Melissa and left. On her way home she met her other workmates.

They were still angry and upset about the way in which Thomas had mistreated Leah earlier, and were very concerned about how this might affect her.

They said to her, "Leah, why don't you report Thomas to the police? Don't worry. We shall go with you as witnesses. We are also tired of his ill-treatment."

"How can I do that?" she asked. "Where will I work if I report him to the police?

Besides, how will my son and I survive?" Leah looked very anxious. "Thomas is the only rich person in this area. Indeed, our only source of survival. Friends, it is late, and my son will be expecting me. I must go now".

"Okay, Leah. See you tomorrow," Leah's workmates said.

Chapter 3 - A song of Sorrow.

The next day, Leah went back to work as usual. As she was digging she spoke and sang of her many sorrows.

Many of her workmates shared these sorrows and some of them wept.

Like the rising ocean waves Leah's lament surged and swelled.

Poverty! Poverty! You are like a disease - so very painful!
You have made my life so hard and miserable.
Tears have become my daily bread.
Poverty! Because of you I have been insulted and humiliated many times.
All my self-respect - you have been taken away!

You have made me eat from the same plate as the pigs.
How long will you make me suffer?
How long will you make me cry?
What kind of a mother am I?
A mother who cannot afford to take her only son to school!

I am tired of you, Poverty!

I curse the day my mother conceived me and the day
when I was born!

"Leah, stop!" Debbie, who was one of Leah's
workmates, interjected.

She then held her hand and consoled her.

"There is always hope after despair, and a good ending
after a painful story. Be strong and hopeful, Leah. Have
faith that, sooner or later, things will be alright.

You are crying today, but tomorrow, you will be a happy
woman."

"Do you know what, Leah?" Debbie asked.

"What?" Leah replied.

"Your son, Andy, and all of us are very proud of you. We
love you, Leah. This should be a big lesson to all of us -
never to treat the needy or poor people the way Thomas
does.

Rather be kind and merciful to those we know and even strangers. By doing so we shall be blessed in many ways. "

While Debbie was still speaking, all the farm and plantation workers came and surrounded Leah.

They shouted together, "Leah! We love you. Be strong! We are in this together."

Deeply moved by Debbie's encouragement and her workmates' support, Leah felt the strength to face the harsh conditions of her daily life.

She smiled and said, "Thank you, Debbie. Thank you everyone."

"You are welcome, friend", they replied.

Unbeknown to Leah and her workmates, Thomas, who was checking crops in a nearby barn and out of sight, was able to hear the whole of this conversation.

Angered by what he felt was a challenge to his authority, he stormed out of the barn and marched towards the workers.

The workers' hearts trembled as he angrily shouted out Leah's name.

"Leah!"

"Yes, sir," Leah replied with trepidation.

"Once poor, always poor!" Thomas said cynically.

"Do you think you will ever be okay, how, tell me?

Trust me, poor woman; you will work for me for as long as you're still strong enough to hold a hoe. If you don't, then you and your son will starve to death."

"I am sorry for everything, sir," Leah said to Thomas in a very low tone.

"Poor woman" said Thomas, and with a look of contempt, Thomas left.

Then Debbie whispered into Leah`s ear, "Well done, Leah. At times we have to apologise - to create peace or to secure a job , even if we know that we are not in the wrong. Don't mind his humiliating words."

"Thank you, Debbie," Leah said.

"You are welcome," she replied.

Chapter 4 - Leah falls sick.

A week later, Leah became ill - very ill.

As time went on her condition worsened.

In her hut she was alone with her nine-year old son, Andy.

Andy felt distressed seeing his mother very sick. He thought of taking her to the hospital, but unfortunately the hospital was many miles away from their home.

For Andy to take his mother to the hospital he needed a car or motorcycle.

Thomas was the only person from Sal Town who owned a car. The other residents didn't even have bicycles.

Andy was not sure what to do. He considered going to Thomas` home to ask for help, but then he remembered how he had humiliated his mother on many occasions.

He shook his head and said, "What can I do?" He then went and sat beside his sick mother.

Andy's eyes were full of tears. He looked at his mother and said, "Just be patient. I will do whatever I can to take you to hospital. You will be okay, mom."

Andy's mother was trying to tell him something, but her words did not come out well. This scared Andy a lot.

He then decided to go to see Thomas to ask for his help. The young boy had no other option.

He held his mother's hand and said to her, "Mom, let me go somewhere. I will come back in a few minutes." Andy then went as fast as he could to Thomas' home.

He found Thomas and his family members sitting in the family car. They were just about to leave to go to their friend's wedding party.

Andy shouted loudly, "Please help me, Mr. Thomas! Please? Please?"

"What is it?" Thomas replied rudely. "I know you want food, but it's not there. Poor boy, go away!"

"No, no, sir," Andy interrupted. "I have not come for food. It's my mother. She is seriously ill. I may lose her unless I take her to the hospital immediately."

The young boy knelt down and begged Thomas, "Please help me to take my mother to the hospital."

"Sorry, I can't help," Thomas replied. "We have an important party to attend and we are already very late."

"Please, sir! Have mercy on me," Andy pleaded. The young boy would not give up.

However the more Andy begged for help, the more angry Thomas became.

"I said I don't have time," Thomas shouted as his anger reached boiling point. "Don't you have ears?" "You want me to take your mother to hospital in my car?"

"Yes, sir," Andy replied.

"Do you have money to put in the fuel?" Thomas interrogated Andy.

"No. But I promise, when I grow up and get a job, I will repay," Andy said meekly.

Thomas' tone changed to mockery. "Andy, as poor as you are, where will you get a job when your mother can't even afford to take you to school? Who will give you a job when you have no qualifications?"

"Okay. I am sorry, sir. But help me and save my mother. Please," Andy pleaded.

Immediately forcing open the car door, and leaping to his feet, Thomas commanded Andy to leave his compound.

"So you think I and my family should miss our friend's wedding party because of your mother? NO WAY!"

Driven by despair and desperation, Andy grabbed Thomas` hand whilst continuing to plead with him.

Exploding with anger, Thomas pushed him away and knocked him to the floor. Thankfully Andy was not injured.

Andy wondered what kind of people Thomas and his family were.

Neither Thomas' wife nor his children got out of the car to help.

"Go away!" Thomas shouted at him. "I'll count to five. If you're still here, then I will break you into pieces."

He started counting.

"One. LEAVE!"

"Two. LEAVE!"

"Three. LEAVE!"

On the fourth count Andy saw that Thomas was determined to hurt him. So he ran away. Thomas then got into his car and drove to the party.

Chapter 5 - Help from friends.

Andy went to the other neighbours, those with whom Leah was working, to see if they could help.

He called out their names loudly. "Please come and help my mother. She is very ill and helpless. She is dying!"

In a few minutes all the neighbours had gathered at Leah`s home. She was in a very bad condition. The neighbours decided that, as none of them owned their own means of transport, to make a stretcher out of bamboo trees.

Fortunately Leah`s home was close to a forest of bamboo trees. Having made the stretcher, they carried Leah on it up to the hospital.

Sadly, on arrival, Leah could neither talk nor breathe well.

Dr. Karl was on duty. He checked Leah and confirmed that she had suffered from pneumonia, which resulted in heart failure.

By now she was in a coma. This sad news broke Andy`s heart, but he resolved to be strong for his mother.

Leah was taken to the ICU, where she received treatment for ten months.

Andy stayed in the hospital, sleeping on the floor near his mother's sick bed. He cared for her with complete dedication during this time.

Every weekend Leah`s workmates walked from their homes to the hospital to check on her and her son. The love and support which they showed them was outstanding.

Chapter 6 - Bad News, Good News.

One day, during the tenth month of Leah's treatment, Andy heard the doctors whispering to each other. They didn't think that anyone could hear them.

However, Andy heard them saying that his mother would not make it.

What he heard upset him deeply. Bursting into tears, he left the room and sat under the tree in the hospital compound.

As he was crying a gentleman called Mr. Rob, who worked in the Office of the President, saw him.

Mr. Rob had just come from a meeting with the Chief Executive Officer (CEO) of Karl International Hospital (KIH).

He asked Andy, "Hey, young boy, what's your name?"

"My name is Andy, sir."

"Okay, Andy, why are you crying? Are you hungry?" Rob asked.

"No, sir," Andy replied.

"Then why are you crying? Please tell me. And by the way, where are your parents?" he insisted.

"Sir, it's about my mother," the young boy said.

"Your mother…has she beaten you?" Mr. Rob was trying to find out why Andy was crying uncontrollably.

Andy thought it was not wise to tell Mr. Rob what he had heard the doctors say: that his mother would not make it.

So he replied. "Sir, my mother is sick, very sick. She has been in a coma for ten months. I can't imagine losing my mother. She's the only one I have in my life. I didn't get a chance to see my father. He died when I was still in my mother's womb."

"Oh, I am sorry to hear that. Well, I can't even imagine what you are going through, but listen to me, Andy. Please stop crying. Okay?"

"Okay, sir," the young boy replied.

Immediately Mr. Rob pulled out a handkerchief from his pocket and wiped the tears from Andy's face. "You have to be strong for your mother, Andy.

Pray for her: that she will be alright."

"Oh, really?" Andy felt hopeful.

"Yes, your mother will be alright," Mr. Rob said.

Although Mr. Rob knew that it would be difficult for someone who had been in a coma for ten months to wake up, he did his best to console Andy.

The conversation continued.

Mr. Rob: "Andy, it's been nice meeting you. My name is Mr. Rob".

Andy: "The pleasure is mine, Mr. Rob."

Mr. Rob: "So is your home nearby?"

Andy: "No, sir. It's very far from here. I come from a small town called Sal."

Mr. Rob: "Oh, that's cool, buddy. I will leave now. But one day I will surely come back to check on you."

Andy: "Alright, sir. Thank you so much for all your kind words."

Mr. Rob: "Okay, goodbye."

Andy: "Bye, sir."

Mr. Rob left. However, when he reached his office, he phoned the Cashiers' Office at the hospital.

He made a commitment to cover the whole of the medical bill for Andy`s mother.

Andy went back to his mother. He held her hand and said, "Mother, how could they?

How could the doctors say that you won't make it? No way! You will be fine. Okay?"

Andy continued to hold his mother's hand for some time. Smiling, he started to sing his favourite song, a song that his mother sang to him when he was growing up.

"*My son, Andy, I love you….*

My son, Andy, I feel so proud of you….

You are everything to me, little prince, Andy!"

As the rhythm of this song grew in strength, like a never-ending fairground ride in his heart, Andy fell asleep.

As he was sleeping, he had a dream. In his dream his mother's face became as real as the noonday sun.

Smiling at him, she asked him for something to eat and a glass of water. Before Andy was able to get food and water for his mother, he woke up.

"Oh! It's just a dream!" he sighed.

After a few minutes had passed, Andy saw something unusual.

His mother's eyes were blinking.

Feeling scared, he left the room and shouted for the doctor's help.

"Doctor, please! I need help."

One of the doctors came out of the office. "Yes, here I am, Andy. What's the problem?

Is everything okay?"

Andy looked pale with fear. "Everything is not okay, doctor," the young boy replied. "My mother needs your help. Her eyes are blinking; I don't know what's going on."

"What? Her eyes are blinking?" the doctor asked.

"Yes, doctor," Andy confirmed.

"That's promising!" The doctor was astonished but nevertheless hopeful.

Leah's eyes were fully open by the time the doctor entered her room.

In the doctor's presence, Leah was able to keep her eyes open for minutes.

Looking at Andy the doctor said, "This is very good."

Andy was speechless. He didn't know what to say. Tears of joy were rolling from his eyes.

"Wow! Look at her fingers, doctor. Are they moving?" Andy wondered.

"Yes, they are," the doctor replied.

"Does this mean that my mother will be able to speak again?" Andy asked.

"Well, Andy, I cannot guarantee that. But there is a possibility that she will," the doctor explained.

"Alright, doctor. Let me try to be patient," Andy said.

"That's a brilliant idea, Andy." The doctor really admired how much Andy cared for and loved his mother.

Chapter 7 - A Prayer.

During the night his mother slept well.

However, Andy tried to get to sleep but he could not.

He kept on checking on his mother.

At four o'clock in the morning, while lying on the floor, he remembered that one of his best friends from a Christian family - his name was Ethan - had once told him that there is a man called Jesus.

This Jesus, he said, is the Son of God whom the Father gave away to die for all mankind, so that whoever believes in Him may not perish but have eternal life.

Ethan explained that Jesus had been very badly treated.

Roman soldiers spat on Him and whipped Him severely before He was crucified on the cross in a place called Golgotha.

While on the cross His hands and feet were pierced with nails.

However, those wounds which brought Him suffering were meant for the healing of all mankind.

Ethan showed Andy a verse from the Bible - *By His stripes we are healed.*

Andy wanted to know more, so Ethan showed him many verses from the Bible, especially those about Jesus' suffering.

Jesus suffered because of His love for us. So we might describe Him as the Saviour, Redeemer, Healer, Deliverer and Protector of men, women and children.

Also, Ethan explained, Jesus was and continues to be a miracle worker.

He is omnipotent, meaning that He is all-powerful. Omniscient means that He is all-knowing. Omnipresent means He is everywhere.

Having remembered this conversation, Andy stood up immediately, knelt on his sick mother's bed and began to pray while holding her hand.

"Dear Jesus,

I really don't know you. I only heard about you from my best friend, Ethan.
Well, my name is Andy.

I am nine years old and the only son of Leah.

I did not get a chance to see my father.

He passed away when my mother was just five months pregnant.

So my mother is everything to me. Yes, she is here fighting for her life, but even before she got sick, she was going through many difficulties.

My wish was to start school when I was four years old, and yet I have not been able to.

My mother cannot afford the school fees.

My friend Ethan goes to school every day and he wants to become a pilot when he's older. I'd be happy to see his dream come true.

I'm hoping that, if my mother gets well, she can take me to school.

If I ever get an opportunity to go to school, my dream is to become a doctor so that I can save lives.

Jesus, is it true that you are omnipotent, omniscient and omnipresent? If you are all-knowing, then you clearly know that my mother has been sick and in a coma for ten months.

You know what she is suffering from and the medicine needed to treat her.

Please forgive me for asking so many questions. Do you know Mr. Thomas, our neighbour at home?

I mean the one who refused to help me and threatened to hurt me?

Well, I forgave him. But if you could visit him and his family, and tell them to change the way they behave, I'd be happy.

Jesus, I ask you to become my friend. I ask you to accept me as well. I ask you to heal and protect my mother. I would like her to speak and walk again. I would like her to see me grow!

I know I have been a disobedient son.

Sometimes she would tell me to go to sleep, but I would not listen to her.

She asked me to help her with the home chores, but I kept on playing.

Nevertheless, she has always given me whatever food she had to share. She has always cared for me.

But from now onwards I promise to change. I promise to be a good child; a child that will make his mother proud.

Andy heard his name being called, "Andy? Andy?"

While Andy was still on his knees praying, he heard someone calling out his name in a low but very clear voice.

The voice was familiar to him. It was his mother!

This was the first time she had spoken in ten months.

Feeling shocked Andy did not know whether to believe he had really heard his mother's voice, or whether he had imagined it.

Too stunned to speak for a minute or so, Andy then replied, "Yes, mom, I am here."

He quickly put the lights on so he could see his mother. She was smiling.

Andy felt too overjoyed merely to return her smile.

Instead he burst into tears: tears of joy!

He then jumped up and down, over and over again, shouting loudly, "It has worked!"

"Trust me, mother. It has worked!" Andy could not stop shouting.

"What has worked, my son?" Leah asked.

"Jesus! Jesus! My mother can speak now! It has worked!"

Leah could not understand what Andy was talking about. She asked again, "Andy, what do you mean? What has worked?"

"Mom, my prayer has worked. It has really worked! Jesus has heard my prayer. He has healed you, mother!"

"What? Has Jesus healed me? Who even taught you about Jesus or how to pray, my son?

This is unbelievable!" Leah said. "Besides, how did I come here? How long have I been here?" she asked.

Everything was new to her. She had never heard about Jesus before.

Indeed, had it not been for his best friend Ethan, even Andy would not have known anything about Him.

Andy then held his mother's hand and explained everything to her: of how Ethan had once told him about Jesus, the son of God; and how their neighbours (workmates) helped him to bring her to the hospital, and how they had been checking on them every weekend.

"Mother, it's now been ten months since we came here.

I have never gone back home.

So today I remembered Ethan telling me about Jesus Christ: that He is a healer and a miracle worker.

Even though I had never prayed before today, I decided to pray for your recovery. I even prayed for Ethan - for his dream to come true.

Also, I prayed and forgave Thomas and his family for trying to hurt me, when I went there to ask for help to bring you to the hospital."

While Andy was still speaking, he saw his mother nodding her head. She could not stop crying.

He asked, "Mother, is everything okay?"

"Yes, son, I now know."

"What? Tell me, Mom," Andy asked politely.

Leah told him that, before she had woken up, she had seen a team of doctors entering her room. Each doctor was dressed in a white and glittering gown.

The senior doctor then came to her bed and started operating on her. After the operation he called her name.

"Leah!"

"Yes, doctor," she replied.

"You are now fine. Everything is okay and your son is eager to see you."

"Where is he?" she asked.

"He is here with us. Just call out his name," the senior doctor replied.

When she called Andy, the team leader left the room together with the other doctors in the team.

Interrupting his mother's account of what she had experienced, Andy said, "Mother, it was Him! I mean Jesus."

"This is unbelievable! It's incredible!" the young boy said.

Holding her son's hand, Leah said, "Andy, I will forever be grateful to Jesus, to you, my son, and my workmates."

Andy thought it was the right time to apologise to his mother. He said to her, "Mum, please forgive me.

I have not been a good child, but now I am a changed person. I promise to be a good listener and a disciplined child."

Leah looked at her son and smiled. "I feel so proud of you, Andy," she said.

"Thank you, mother, I am proud of you too," he replied.

So Andy and his mother accepted Jesus Christ as their friend, healer and protector. "We shall tell this story to everyone we come across!" they declared.

Then Andy rushed immediately to the doctors and nurses, shouting, "my friend has operated on and healed my mother. She is now fine!

Discharge us and we shall go home."

The doctors could not believe Andy. "Young boy, are you crazy?" one of the doctors asked.

"No! I am not, doctor." Andy quickly defended himself. "Come and check on my mother. She can now speak well."

"Impossible!" one of the doctors said while rushing to Leah's room.

They found Leah smiling. Dr. Karl immediately called her name.

"Leah?"

"Yes, Doctor."

"Impossible!" Dr. Karl said.

"How can this be possible?" - a question he asked several times. He was really shocked.

"What happened, Leah?" He was trying to understand how such a sudden transformation could have occurred..

Although Dr. Karl was trying to remain calm, while assessing Leah's medical condition, he could not hold back his tears. He kept on repeating, "Impossible! Impossible!"

As Dr. Karl and his team tried to help Leah to get out of her bed, Leah told them, "It's okay. I can do it myself."

"What? This is unbelievable!" another of the doctors exclaimed; and the rest of the doctors in the team agreed.

While Leah was getting out of bed, many other members of the medical staff, and even some of the patients, gathered to see her.

As Leah and Andy took it in turns to narrate the whole story, a silence descended on the ward.

Those listening were both awed and amazed.

It was difficult to take in - surely such an extraordinary transformation never happened in real life?

But the evidence was clear to see - Leah, whose life had been hanging in the balance - for whom any hope of recovery seemed remote and elusive, was now fully alert and well, and able to speak eloquently and with great confidence.

After Leah and Andy had shared their story, the doctors and nurses carried out various tests and scans.

The results all came out negative. Leah's health condition was completely normal.

"Well, I call this a miracle." Dr. Karl concluded. "Andy?"

"Yes, doctor?"

"I think you should introduce me to your friend, Jesus. He is indeed a great Doctor; a doctor above all doctors."

Everyone was impressed by this outstanding miracle.

They had witnessed Leah waking up and speaking coherently. In the course of time every person came to accept Jesus Christ as their friend and saviour.

Before leaving the hospital premises, Leah and Andy were asked to go to the cashier's office to pay the medical bill. Leah was in a panic, wondering how she was going to get the money to clear the bill.

To their great surprise the cashier gave them receipts on arrival. "Who paid the bill?" Leah asked.

The cashier replied that a man called Mr. Rob had cleared the bill.

"What?" Leah and her son exclaimed together.

"But who is Mr. Rob, and where does he come from?" Leah kept asking.

"Mr. Rob works in the Office of the President," the Cashier clarified.

"Office of the President?" Leah looked confused.

"Wait. I know Mr. Rob. I've just remembered!" Andy said.

"Andy, stop!" Leah raised her voice to Andy.

"Mother, trust me. I know him. He is my friend. He found me crying and consoled me. He told me to be strong for your sake, and to pray for you. However, he did not tell me that he was going to clear the bill."

Both Leah and the cashier were surprised. They didn't know that Andy had met Mr. Rob in person.

"And another thing, Mother," Andy said. "Let me whisper it into your ear. Mr. Rob promised me that he will come to check on me one day."

"What? Is that true, Andy?" Leah could not believe what her son told her.

"Yes! It's true, mammy," Andy confirmed.

"What are you talking about?" The cashier was eager to know.

"Nothing," Leah and Andy replied at once.

Leah and Andy then went to Dr. Karl's office, to extend their sincere appreciation to him for all of his kindness to them.

Noticing that they were about to get onto their knees to say thank you, he said quickly, "Please don't. It's okay."

Remaining on their feet, but nevertheless wanting to express their appreciation in some way, they felt they could convey this in words. "Thank you so much, Dr. Karl. You have been so kind to us." They spoke together and smiled.

"You are welcome," he replied.

Dr. Karl thanked Andy for caring for his mother. He said, "I am a doctor, and I have been the CEO of this hospital for twenty-one years but since its inception, I have never seen someone of your age taking care of their mother with the dedication and commitment you have shown.

Thank you so much, Andy.

I really respect and admire you for that. And from today, if you ever need someone to talk to, I want you to know that my door is always open. Please take my business card with you."

"Oh. My goodness! Thank you, Dr. Karl," Andy said.

After chatting for a few minutes, Dr. Karl had to leave to attend an urgent meeting. Leah and Andy said goodbye and left the hospital with big smiles on their faces.

Chapter 8 - A Question.

The news about Leah`s miraculous recovery was spoken about in every household within the town of Sal.

Most of the residents had lost hope that she would ever recover. They were overjoyed to hear that she was now well and able to return home.

On the day of her return home, Leah's workmates gathered at her home to welcome her.

They brought food which they cooked and ate together.

Leah thanked them for their warm welcome, and for the love they had shown both before and during the time she had spent in the hospital.

"I will forever be grateful to you all," she said.

However, the story did not end there.

Mr. Rob had heard the good news about the recovery of Andy's mother from Dr. Karl.

Although he was happy to hear the good news he was, nevertheless, astonished and somewhat incredulous - could such a miracle really happen?

Did miracles ever happen?

Chapter 9 - A Surprise Visitor.

A month later he decided to drive to Sal town, to find out how Andy and his mother were getting on.

On arriving in Sal, he asked one of the residents where he could find Leah's home.

An old man asked him, "You mean Leah who miraculously got healed and has a son called Andy?"

"Yes, sir," Mr. Rob replied.

Then the old man gave him directions. Andy was at home. However, Leah was not there.

Now that she was strong enough, she was working at Thomas' plantation again.

On seeing the condition of the building in which Andy and Leah lived, which had very few resources and amenities, Mr. Rob started to feel sad and slightly tearful.

"Anyone here?" he asked.

Andy was sleeping inside the hut. He felt hungry because food prices had been rising, and both he and his mother had only had very meagre meals during the previous few days.

"Hello? Is anyone here?" Mr. Rob asked again.

Waking from his sleep, Andy said, "Sorry for keeping you waiting. Let me come out."

On opening the door, he recognised Mr. Rob immediately.

Smiling, he said, "Mr. Rob, I am so happy to see you, sir!"

"I am happy to see you too, buddy," Mr. Rob replied.

Having invited Mr. Rob to come in, Andy brought him an old mat to sit on, as they did not have any chairs at home.

"Sir," he said. "Please have a seat."

"Thank you, Andy," Mr. Rob said.

"You are welcome, sir." He got down on his knees and said, "Sir, thank you very much for paying our hospital bill. And…"

Before Andy had an opportunity to add anything further, Mr. Rob interrupted him.

Holding out his hand to Andy, he said, "You don't need to kneel down for me. Please stand up. It's okay, Andy."

After a pause of a few seconds, he continued speaking. "Where is your mother?" he asked.

Andy sighed. "My mother left in the morning to work at Thomas' plantation."

"That's awesome. I'm glad she has a job," Mr. Rob said. "Is she okay?"

"Not exactly," Andy replied. Tears started to well up in his eyes.

"Oh, I am sorry. I didn't mean to hurt or offend you, Andy," Mr. Rob apologised.

"Sir, please don't be sorry," Andy reassured Mr. Rob. "This is not about you. It's about my mother."

"What's the problem?" he asked.

Although Andy was still upset, he struggled to regain composure.

He wanted to make sure Mr. Rob understood his mother's situation; indeed, *their* situation.

"You see, my mother has been working at Thomas` home for many years now.

However, Thomas mistreats her a lot. Every time she goes there, she returns home crying."

Andy paused. He found it difficult to speak.

It was painful for him to speak of his mother's suffering. After a minute's pause he continued.

"Sometimes he doesn't pay her. At other times he cuts off her pay for no reason.

But she cannot sue him because he is the only rich person in the area, and no one else could provide her with a job.

Just before my mother got sick, and went to Karl International hospital, Thomas had beaten her very badly."

"What! Why did he do that?" Mr. Rob exclaimed. He felt shocked.

"Well, my mother and I often sleep on an empty stomach as we don't get enough food to eat.

Unfortunately, at Thomas' home, not only my mother, but also other workers, are not given lunch. Yet they have to work for long hours.

That day my mother was very hungry and had serious ulcers.

She ran to Thomas' wife for help, but she chased her away, saying there was no free food.

My mother did not have a choice. She went to the pigs' house where she ate the leftovers.

While she was still eating, Thomas saw her. He quickly grabbed a big stick and hit my mother several times."

"What? Is that true?" Mr. Rob exclaimed.

"It's true, sir," Andy confirmed.

"To be honest with you, sir, my mother doesn't go there because she wants to.

There is not any other work which my mother has, and so she must go there. Otherwise, we don't eat.

What hurts her most is that she can't afford to pay for me to go to school.

All my friends in the neighbourhood are at school. But I still have hope and faith that one day I will go to school."

Mr. Rob struggled to hold back his tears while listening to this sad story.

Wiping away his tears, he asked. "Andy, what would you like to be in the future, if given a chance to go to school?"

"A doctor," Andy replied swiftly.

"Okay then, Andy. I will make sure that your dream comes true."

Mr. Rob's manner was confident and Andy could see that he meant what he said.

This was no idle promise.

"Sir, do you really mean that?" Andy asked hopefully, but with a tremor of doubt in his voice.

"Yes, Andy. I really mean it," Mr. Rob said in a solemn and calm manner.

Uncertain whether he might be dreaming, Andy took a moment or two to think about what Mr. Rob had said.

Could this really be true? But, yes, it really must be true!

Like the slight rustle of a bird's wing, hope began to stir in his heart; but then, like a peacock fully unfolding its plumes, the joy he felt could no longer be contained, but burst forth.

In an explosion of excitement the young boy jumped up and down, over and over again.

Hugging Mr. Rob, he said, "Sir, I will never disappoint you.

I will be a good boy, both at home and at school. I will read hard, so that I become one of the best students in the school.

Thank you so much."

"No problem." Mr. Rob was delighted to see how Andy's mood had brightened.

A few minutes later Leah arrived, carrying a hoe on her shoulder. She was very tired and exhausted. Her dress was worn and tattered, and her feet bare and dirty.

Her hands were also calloused and dirty with over-work.

Seeing Mr. Rob smiling at her, Leah felt very embarrassed, as she was dishevelled and dirty.

She was afraid to shake hands with him.

However, she welcomed him with a beautiful smile.

"Mom, he is the one," Andy interjected.

"What do you mean, Andy?" Leah asked.

She had never seen Mr. Rob before.

"He is Mr. Rob, a friend of mine who cleared our bill," Andy revealed.

"Is that true, sir?" Leah asked Mr. Rob in a rather incredulous tone.

"Yes ma`am. My name is Mr. Rob. I work in the Office of the President."

"Oh my goodness!" Leah was thrilled. "You are most welcome here, sir," she said.

"Thank you," he replied.

Leah tried to get down onto her knees to thank Mr. Rob for clearing the bill. However, Mr. Rob quickly stopped her.

"Leah, please don't. It's okay."

"Thank you so much, sir," she said.

"You're welcome, Leah," he replied.

"So how long have you been here?" Leah asked.

"For just for an hour," Mr. Rob replied.

Turning towards Andy, Leah asked, "Andy, why didn't you call me?

At least I would have come and made some tea for Mr. Rob, even though we have no sugar or bread in the house."

"I am sorry, mother," Andy replied. "Mr. Rob asked me not to. He said he would wait until you arrived back home."

Leah felt a little more reassured; although, with a mildly concerned expression, she turned to speak to Mr. Rob.

"Oh, you must be hungry, sir."

"Don't mind, Leah. I am fine," he replied.

Mr. Rob could tell by Andy's facial expression that he was very hungry, although Andy tried hard to disguise his feelings.

Mr. Rob was very concerned about him and his mother.

After a few moments of reflection, he said. "Leah and Andy: Tomorrow I want you to go with me somewhere. I will be here to pick you up at eight o'clock in the morning. Please be ready by that time."

Leah: "Sir, where do you want us to go with you?"

Mr. Rob: "It is a surprise, Leah."

Leah: "Anyway, thank you, Mr. Rob, but maybe only Andy will go with you."

Mr. Rob: "But what about you, Leah?"

Leah: "I will be at Thomas' place for work. I cannot go anywhere without his permission. If I insist and go, then I may lose my job, or if not my job then this week's pay."

Mr. Rob: "Leah, from today you will not go back to work there.

Andy has already told me about what you are going through.

I will do what I can to support you and your son. And one more thing, next year Andy will start going to school."

"What?" Leah interjected out of shock.

"Yes, I mean it," Mr. Rob confirmed.

On hearing this good news, Leah stopped worrying about the dirty clothes she was wearing.

She opened her arms wide and hugged Mr. Rob.

"I really appreciate your help. Thank you so much, sir," she said.

"You are very welcome," Mr. Rob replied.

Overwhelmed by happiness and excitement, Leah started to cry.

Then Mr. Rob said to her, "Leah, what you and your son have gone through is enough.

You now deserve to live a decent life."

Glancing at his watch, he continued, "Oh, it's getting late. I am sorry I have to go now.

See you all tomorrow."

"Okay, sir. We pray you reach home safely." Waving their hands together in unison, Andy and Leah wished Mr. Rob a good night.

Mr. Rob got into his car and left.

Andy commented to his mother that his friend Jesus must have heard everything he prayed for during their time together in the hospital.

"That's true, son. Otherwise, how could this happen?" Leah agreed.

"How could someone from the Office of the President visit us, out of all the people in this town? Anyway, let's see whether he does what he has promised us.

But, of course, he will be here tomorrow." Leah spoke with confidence. She did not doubt Mr. Rob.

"Wow! I can't wait, mother," Andy said.

"Okay. Let us sleep so that we're ready in the morning," Leah suggested.

"Okay, good night, mother."

"Good night, son."

Chapter 10. - A Shopping Trip.

In the morning, while Andy and his mother were getting ready, they heard a car horn hooting in their compound. Andy went outside and looked at the car.

A man got out. It was none other than Mr. Rob.

Smiling at Mr. Rob, Andy said, "Good morning, sir."

"Good morning, Andy," Mr. Rob replied, returning Andy's smile. "Where is your mother? Is she ready?"

Before Andy had time to reply, Leah came out and greeted Mr. Rob. "Thank you, sir, for keeping your word."

"It's okay, Leah. Please get into the car and we can go."

As they were moving through the streets of Sal town, all of the local people who knew Leah could not believe it when they saw her sitting comfortably with Andy in a Mercedes Benz car.

"How is this possible? Is this the Leah that we know, or is she someone else? And who is that gentleman?

Where are they going?" The residents wondered.

"Oh, if Leah can sit in such a car, then no hard situation is permanent," one of the residents commented.

It was not only a marvel to the residents of Sal town, but also to Leah and her son.

It was the first time they had travelled or sat in a car.

Mr. Rob drove them to a city which was about three hours' drive away.

They had never visited this city before. Everything was new to them.

He then took them to a good restaurant for lunch. "Please feel free and ask for any food you'd like to eat," he said.

Smiling, and delighted by the excellence of the hospitality provided, Andy and his mother ordered their food.

The waiter who served them brought a variety of food and drinks. They ate and drank with joyful hearts until they had eaten enough.

After they had completed their meal, Mr. Rob took them to the biggest shopping mall in the city.

He bought them enough clothes and shoes to meet their needs on any occasion.

He also bought other items for them to use at home, including mattresses, bed sheets and blankets, because they had both been sleeping on rugs.

After shopping he took them to a zoo where they saw their favourite animals.

Very happy and excited, but also a little tired, they enjoyed the ride home with Mr. Rob in the late afternoon.

"Thank you so much for your generosity, sir. What a trip!" both Leah and Andy said to Mr. Rob.

Mr. Rob was pleased to hear that they had enjoyed their day.

"I am glad you have both enjoyed the trip, "he said.

It was about 8 o'clock at night when they arrived at Leah and Andy's home in Sal Town.

Before leaving and saying good-bye, Mr. Rob gave them some money to buy food, and other essential household items, sufficient to last for a few months.

He promised to always visit them, whenever he had a holiday from work. He wanted to make sure that they were well and not in want of anything.

Chapter 11. - A Party.

At home Leah's life changed completely.

Andy and his mother were no longer sleeping on empty stomachs. But, most importantly, Leah stopped working at Thomas' place.

This change brought her peace of mind.

Leah had a strikingly attractive figure as well as personality.

She had the confidence of a strong, athletic man but, at the same time, the demureness of a woman who is completely centred in God.

Mr. Rob continued to support both Leah and Andy.

On most weekends he would take them out for dinner.

As time went on he started to fall in love with Leah.

Mr. Rob, who had never been married before, was forty-eight years old.

Leah was forty-five years old.

Even though his love for Leah was strong, he was not sure whether she would accept his marriage proposal.

Working together with his fellow members of staff, he arranged a surprise birthday party for Andy, when he would have an opportunity to propose to Leah.

One of Mr. Rob's friends made a phone call to Leah.

"Hello?"

"Yes?" Leah replied.

"Am I speaking to Leah?"

"Yes, who is this?" Leah felt anxious.

"I am Keith, a friend and colleague of Mr. Rob."

"What? Is he okay?" Leah interrupted.

"No. He is not," he replied.

"Oh, no! What happened?" she asked.

"Well, it's hard to tell unless you come and see him yourself."

"Where exactly should I come?" Leah asked.

Keith had phoned when he was already on the way to pick up Leah and Andy. As Leah was leaving her home, she saw a car coming towards her.

Keith got out of the car and said, "Are you Leah?"

"Yes I am," she replied.

"Where is your son?" he asked.

"I have left him at home."

No! He needs to come with us. Mr. Rob wants to see him."

A few moments later Leah returned to Keith's car, now accompanied by Andy.

Looking very nervous as they got into Keith's car, Leah kept on saying loudly, "I hope Mr. Rob is okay."

"Mother, don't worry. Our friend Jesus will protect him. Nothing bad will happen to him."

Andy consoled his mother while holding her hand.

Keith could clearly see the love and care which Leah and Andy had for Mr. Rob.

However, he did not mention anything to them. He just drove them up to the venue.

Just after Andy and Leah and Keith arrived at the venue, everyone started to sing:

Happy birthday to you,
Happy birthday to you,
Happy birthday, dear Andy…
Happy birthday to you!

Andy`s mother had never had the opportunity or the resources to organise a birthday party for Andy, although she had always wished him a happy birthday and made him a cake.

This was the very first time that a birthday party had ever been held in Andy's honour.

Both Andy and Leah felt overwhelmed and burst into tears.

As Leah was wiping away Andy`s tears, she noticed a very handsome man, dressed in a neatly tailored dark blue business suit.

Holding a bunch of roses in his right hand, and with a very big smile, he was walking towards her while members of the audience were clapping.

Guess who he was? Mr. Rob!

He gave the roses to Leah and gently pulled out a gold ring from the right-hand pocket of his jacket.

Then he immediately got down onto his knees and proposed. "Leah, will you marry me?"

"Wow! What a surprise!" Leah's eyes glistened with delight.

She looked at her son, and Andy said to her, "Mom, it's okay."

Leah remained quiet for about two minutes, but then, smiling at Mr. Rob, she said, "Yes! I will."

It was a joyful moment which words cannot describe.

Mr. Rob gave Leah an engagement ring and hugged her. Leah and Mr. Rob then took Andy by his hands and showed him his birthday cake.

Andy cut it into slices and gave the first portions to them, and then the rest of the portions to everyone else at the party.

There was a variety of food and drink at the party and everyone enjoyed themselves.

The party was a great success. Everything went exactly as planned.

When the party had finished, Mr. Rob drove Leah and Andy back home. Leah and Mr. Rob married a few months later.

Chapter 12 - A Wedding and a Speech.

The wedding was attended by many prominent people, especially those who knew Mr. Rob, amongst whom was the president, the head of state.

Towards the end of his wedding speech, Mr. Rob asked Andy to accept his gift for him.

This was an envelope containing adoption papers.

When Andy opened it, and saw what it was about, he accepted Mr. Rob as his dad without any hesitation.

He already looked upon Mr. Rob as a father, as he knew him to be a good and caring person.

Following tradition, Leah was given a chance to say a word, but she was speechless with joy.

All she could do was cry.

She couldn't hold back her tears of joy.

But what really amazed her, Mr. Rob and the audience was that Andy then raised his hand and asked for a microphone from the master of ceremonies.

He had prepared his own speech.

He was a confident young boy who knew how to both speak and write.

Even though he had never been to school, his best friend Ethan had been coming over to Leah and Andy's home every evening and every weekend, to teach Andy whatever he was studying at school.

Ethan was a very able teacher - although just a boy without any formal training in teaching and Andy was a very quick and able student.

Andy began his speech.

"Good evening to you all.

My name is Andy. In fact I didn't want to talk, but since my mother could not talk, let me do so on her behalf.

I must confess that, ever since Mr. Rob came into our lives, things have changed completely.

It actually made me think that bad things happen at times to open up new opportunities.

Had it not been for my mother's admission to Karl International hospital Mr. Rob would not have met us.

Therefore I want to encourage each and everyone going through hardships not to be shaken or to fear. Those hardships you are in now are maybe paving a way for you to your destiny.

Just be patient. Be hopeful and have faith.

It's what helped my mother and I to face and endure all the conditions we suffered until Mr. Rob came into our lives.

My mother is a living testimony.

People of Sal town know that, if it's suffering, she has suffered. If it's humiliation, she has been humiliated.

If it's eating pigs' food, she has done so, if it's going to sleep hungry, she has done this all too often.

Nevertheless, there is a time for everything. There is a time to cry and a time to feel joy and happiness. Mother, who knew this day would happen? You have a reason to smile mammy. This is your day!

As for me, Mr. Rob, I feel I don't have the right words to use to extend my sincere appreciation to you. Just know that, from the bottom of my heart, I am thankful for everything you have done for us.

I promise - before everyone here -that I will be a good son. I will never disappoint you. Never!

Mammy and dad, I love you both very much and I wish you a happy and blessed marriage. Thank you."

Everyone in the audience was impressed by Andy's eloquence and the depth and sincerity of his love for both Leah and Mr. Rob.

Many were quietly crying, even the President and Leah's former boss, Thomas.

It was one of those rare speeches which people would never be able to forget, and Andy was just nine years old!

Later, the couple cut their cake and served it to everyone.

Everyone commented how delicious the cake tasted.

Chapter 13 - Life moves on for Andy.

Leah found it hard to believe that her life had changed so suddenly - from struggling to survive in a ramshackle house to living comfortably in a beautiful house.

Andy's life had changed suddenly as well.

He was now a student at one of the best schools in the city - Lark International School.

He would never forget his first day there.

He felt nervous and excited at the same time.

At Lark International School children started in Kindergarten and then progressed to High School.

However, having interviewed and tested Andy, the teaching staff recognized that he had sufficient ability, knowledge and skills to be able to start straight away in the fourth grade.

Andy felt very thankful to his best friend Ethan, who had been a very faithful coach and from whom he had learned much.

Andy knew that, had it not been for Ethan's support, he would have failed the school's interview.

Andy had promised his parents that he would always work hard - that he would do his best and try to achieve the best scores.

With unfailing perseverance he achieved his goal.

In his end-of-term assessment he obtained the highest scores in class.

By working very hard, and with the support of his teachers and fellow students, he was able to achieve success.

Lark International School was not just a school; it was also a second home to Andy - a place where he felt accepted, safe and happy.

He was dependable and trustworthy as well as neat and academically excellent.

The school principal was so impressed by Andy's meticulous attention to detail that he decided to appoint him as a prefect.

It was a role which Andy loved to the very core of his being, and in which he served for the whole of his school career.

He completed whatever task was assigned to him with zeal and untiring commitment.

He was very popular with, and well-respected by, all of the students.

He was approachable but never showed partiality or favouritism. He always sought to treat others fairly.

His performance in the final exams was excellent.

He was now eager and ready to join the University.

Mr. Rob and Leah had been planning to pay Andy's University tuition fees.

However, they shared Andy's joy when he told them some very good news: he had been awarded a scholarship to study a degree in Medicine and Surgery at the University of Garten.

It took him five years to complete the course.

He achieved first class honours and then undertook further training to become a pulmonologist which is a physician who specialises in treatment of the respiratory system.

Humility, determination and hardwork were keys to Andy's ongoing success.

Within a few years he was offered a job at the University of Garten as a senior lecturer in Medicine.

He became one of the most well-paid lecturers at the University.

He also worked at Karl International Hospital.

Chapter 14 - Thomas shows up.

One day, when Dr. Andy was on duty at the hospital, an ambulance brought in a patient who was in a critical condition.

The patient's family members were crying out for help.

It was such a surprise for Dr. Andy to discover that the new patient was Thomas, Leah's previous employer!

There is a pattern and a purpose in life, although the outworking of this is often not recognised at the time.

The Thomas who mistreated Leah, the same Thomas who refused to help Andy to take his mother to the hospital, had come to a hospital where Mr. Rob was one of the Board members and the doctor who happened to be on duty that day was Leah's son.

Thomas' wife and children, who on many occasions had refused to help Leah, were now crying out for help from Leah's son.

They did not recognise Dr. Andy, as the last occasion on which they had seen him was when he was just a boy.

Andy had left Sal town when he was just nine years old.

He had completed all of his studies in the city.

During the school holidays he stayed with his parents at another town called Ndon, which was about one hour's drive from Sal.

On seeing them get out of the ambulance, Andy remembered Thomas, his wife and children.

He ordered the nurses to take Thomas to the ICU.

The medical staff carried out tests, which showed that Thomas' kidneys had failed.

Thomas would need a kidney transplant, if he was to have a realistic hope of leading a long and happy life.

The medical staff also found out that Thomas was anaemic and had the rarest blood type, AB negative, which was not matched by that of any of his family members.

None of the blood supplies available at the hospital matched it either.

As it happened, Dr. Andy`s blood group was AB negative.

Without hesitation he volunteered to donate blood to Thomas.

Thomas, who had been very unwell when he had been brought into hospital, started to improve, although he was still unable to recognise anyone, including his wife and children.

Doctors Andy and Karl told the family members to look for a living donor; someone on whom they could operate, to remove one of their kidneys, so it could be transplanted into the patient.

The family members looked for a donor, but could not find anyone.

Even though the family had enough money to pay whichever person offered to become a donor, no one came forward.

There were some people who may have been able to help, but they chose not to, because Thomas and his family were notorious in Sal town for their arrogance and ruthlessness.

It seems that everyone was tired of them.

As time passed, Thomas's wife and children became very worried.

The longer the delay, the more Thomas' health condition deteriorated.

The doctors tried other treatments, but nothing helped him.

Thomas' family was at breaking point and almost felt like giving into despair - they had tried their best and failed.

Dr. Andy did not tell his parents that the patient who needed a kidney transplant was Thomas.

However, he told them that he was going to help, as the family had failed to find a living donor.

At first his parents were very worried about his decision, but later on they realised that Andy should follow his heart, and so gave him their blessing.

As soon as Dr. Andy had told Dr. Karl of his decision, Dr. Karl called Thomas` wife into his office.

He told her that someone was willing to become Thomas' donor.

"Who is this person, Doctor?" she asked politely.

"One of our doctors here," he replied.

"Don't mind, Doctor. We are ready to pay whatever amount of money he or she asks," she promised.

Dr. Karl asked a well-known specialist friend to do the operation and thankfully the operation was successful.

Following the operation Thomas` health condition started to improve significantly.

Eventually he was fully well and ready to be discharged.

He could now speak perfectly and walk by himself.

Thomas then asked his wife who the donor was.

"One of the doctors here," she confirmed. "He is so kind and polite.

He also volunteered to donate blood to you on the first day we came here."

"Did he tell you his name?" Thomas asked.

"No, he did not." His wife replied.

"I will not leave this hospital before I speak to him.

I want to know who he is and also to thank him in person." Thomas was eager to know.

Dr. Andy was not at the hospital on this particular day.

He was at the University teaching the Medical students, but Thomas kept on wondering about this good Samaritan who had saved his life. Indeed, had it not been for Dr. Andy`s intervention, Thomas would have died.

The next day, Dr. Andy came to the hospital as usual.

He then went to Thomas` room to check how he was doing.

"How are you, Thomas?" he asked.

"I am fine, doctor. I really now feel okay," he replied with a smile.

As they were still speaking together, Dr. Karl came in with Thomas` wife.

"Oh, Thomas, you have been asking who donated a kidney to you. He is the one."

"Who, doctor?" Thomas asked politely

Dr. Karl pointed at Dr. Andy.

"Yes, I am the one, Mr. Thomas," Andy confirmed.

Thomas stood up immediately and hugged Dr. Andy.

He thanked him for saving his life. "Doctor, I will forever be grateful to you.

May you live longer, to save many more lives!"

Thomas then asked his wife to pass him the gift they had prepared for Dr. Andy.

It was a big envelope containing thousands of bank notes.

He said to Andy, "Doctor, I know this can't repay you for what you did for me, but kindly accept it. It's a small gift from me and my family."

"Don't mind, Mr. Thomas. It's okay."

Dr. Andy did not accept the gift.

"But how can I extend my sincere appreciation to you, doctor?" Thomas insisted - he wanted Dr. Andy to take the money.

Thomas," Andy said. "My parents taught me to be kind to everyone, both those I know and who love me, but even the strangers; and to give without expectation of the kindness being returned."

"One's life is so much more important than any amount of money.

I am thrilled that I was able to help you, and you are now well. That's a sufficient reward for me, Thomas."

"My son, your parents must be proud of you!" Thomas said with tears rolling from his eyes. "Doctor, please come to see us when you have time.

You are very welcome to join my family and I for dinner."

Dr. Andy was happy to accept Thomas' invitation.

"But what's your name, doctor?" Thomas' wife asked. "And may we have your phone number, if that's okay with you?"

"Oh, yes! Please do," Thomas agreed.

"Okay, my name is Dr. Andy," Dr. Andy confirmed.

"What?" Thomas interjected, with a rather shocked and bewildered expression. "Dr. Andy? Who are your parents?"

"I am a son to Leah and Mr. Rob, who works in the office of the President," Dr. Andy confirmed.

"What?" Thomas and his wife said together.

They both looked stunned, rather like someone who has been temporarily dazed by bright car lights shining in the dark.

Thomas knew Mr. Rob, and that he was married to Leah, because he had attended their wedding.

However, he did not know that Andy had trained to become a doctor, nor did he know the name of the owner and manager of the hospital in which he was receiving treatment!

Overcome by shock, Thomas fainted.

His wife, also shocked and afraid, fell on her knees immediately, and begged Dr. Andy to forgive them for everything they had done to him and his mother.

Dr. Karl was shocked.

He had heard about Thomas from Dr. Andy, but he did not know that this patient was the same person as the Thomas whom Andy had known when he was a boy.

He was amazed to discover all that Dr. Andy had done to save Thomas' life, despite all the bad things he had done to him and his mother.

Dr. Karl hugged Andy and said, "We are proud of you, Dr. Andy.

I know your parents will be so happy to hear this. You are an outstanding son and doctor!"

When Thomas had recovered consciousness, and with tears streaming from his eyes, he quickly grabbed Dr. Andy's right hand and said, "I don't deserve forgiveness. But I beg of you, Doctor, please forgive me!"

"I have already forgiven you, Mr. Thomas." Dr. Andy said.

"Thank you, doctor. Thank you so much!" Thomas was overjoyed.

"You are welcome," Dr. Andy replied.

Thomas felt ashamed of his former way of life; of the many times he had been ruthless and unkind towards his neighbours.

"Dr. Andy," he said. "I have hurt many people, including your mother.

I don't even know whether she will ever forgive me, but I promise to change into a new and decent person.

This is a very big lesson! If you had wanted, you could have left me to die, but thankfully you did not.

Instead you showed me love and compassion."

Chapter 15 - A transformation.

Having been discharged from the hospital, Thomas returned home with his wife and children.

He arranged a thanksgiving party for the following week, to which he invited Dr. Andy and his parents and all the residents of Sal Town.

Everyone to whom Thomas had either spoken or written accepted his invitation.

They all enjoyed the party and ate and drank until they were full.

"This is so strange. It's very hard to believe," one of the residents commented.

Indeed, it was strange, because no one had ever eaten anything at Thomas` home before.

This time he encouraged everyone to eat and drink as much as they wanted.

"Thomas is a changed man - a new man.

He's an entirely different person from the one we used to know.""

Observations such as this and comments made using different words, but with much the same meaning, were whispered by one neighbour to another.

Most neighbours had something to say, but even the few who said nothing silently agreed with those who had spoken.

Dr. Andy and his parents had been delayed and so left their home much later than they had intended.

Thomas was eagerly waiting for them.

However, he was beginning to lose hope that they would come.

As he was about to begin a speech, which he had been working on for several days, he saw a Mercedes Benz car with tinted windows coming into the compound.

Accompanied by his wife he approached the car to see who it belonged to.

As he did so, Dr. Andy and his parents got out.

Thomas and his wife welcomed them and directed them to their seats.

The couple and their son were elegantly attired. They looked very smart and neat.

Even though the residents immediately recognised Leah and her husband, they did not remember Andy until Thomas introduced him.

Thomas began his speech by welcoming everyone and thanking them for coming.

He wanted to give special recognition to Dr. Andy, and so he asked him to stand up.

Smiling at Andy, and then at everyone in the audience, he said, "Dr. Andy is a son to Mr. Rob and Leah.

He is now a medical doctor who works at Karl International Hospital.

He is also a lecturer in medicine at the University of Garten."

"Wonderful!" The residents shouted with joy and happiness.

They found it hard to believe the good news.

Then Thomas proceeded to narrate the whole story of how Dr. Andy had saved his life when he went to the hospital in a critical condition.

"If it hadn't been for him, I would be dead by now," he said in an awed and solemn tone.

He glanced at Leah who was silently crying. "Madam Leah," he said. "I understand you have many reasons not to forgive my family - especially me!

But I ask you to forgive me."

"Your son not only saved my life.

He also taught me that one's life is more important than money.

I have learned a lot from your son, Madam Leah.

Dr. Andy has taught me how to love and help other people, without expecting to receive anything in return - without 'strings attached'.

He has taught me how to respect and care for others, and to be compassionate and kind."

Leah continued to cry as Thomas made his confession.

She reflected on all she had gone through: the suffering and the shame; but finally she found the courage to forgive Thomas and his family.

She announced, in a voice resonating with confidence and hope, "I have forgiven you everything, Mr. Thomas."

"Thank you, Madam Leah." Thomas' voice was tremulous with emotion.

This story shocked the residents.

They would never have expected Dr. Andy to help Thomas, as they knew how badly he had treated Andy's mother and how he had threatened to hurt Andy the time he asked him for help when his mother was seriously sick.

An awed silence fell upon every person present and Thomas began to speak more loudly.

"My fellow residents and employees, I ask you to forgive me as well.

I pledge to pay you all the money which I owe you.

From today I will give all of those of you who work for me free lunches and allowances."

Every employee was then amazed when Thomas, assisted by all of his family members, gave each of them an envelope containing money.

This was to compensate them for the reductions made to their pay over many years.

Thomas had also added on additional payments, to bring their wages up to a fair market rate.

Leah was especially pleased, as Thomas had given her all of the money she had demanded when she was still working at his banana plantation.

Leah rejoiced to see this transformation in Mr. Thomas and in her own circumstances.

"Someone who on so many occasions has called me a poor woman now calls me Madam.

He has even paid me my arrears! This is unbelievable!" she said.

Indeed, it was hard to believe.

All of Thomas `employees were overjoyed to see this transformation in Thomas.

Finally he had made reparation to them for the many years of suffering they had experienced because of his cruel treatment.

It was a time of reconciliation, peace and happiness.

The party ended well.

And so Thomas changed completely.

He started to treat his employees, and everyone with whom he came into contact with love and respect.

He helped anyone who came to him in need.

Chapter 15 - Charitable donations.

The transformation in Thomas bore fruit in so many ways, not least of which was the transformation in the lives of the many people who knew him.

Leah was one of these beneficiaries.

She used the money she had received from Thomas to start a non governmental organisation.

She named it the Leah and Family Foundation - an organisation which helps and works with single mothers and all the needy families in Sal Town.

It's now fifteen years since Leah first founded it.

Every month Leah and Family Foundation receives more than fifty volunteers, with expertise in various areas, from countries from all over the world.

The volunteers help to train the beneficiaries in a broad range of skills, focused on making crafts goods of various kinds such as table and sleeping mats, baskets, bags, beads and necklaces, bangles and bracelets and much more besides.

The income generating activities help many families in Sal town to earn a living because there is always a customer for the items they make.

Some of the crafts goods are sold to tourists or visitors, while others are sold to a local craft shop which was owned by a husband and wife from Germany.

Families in Sal no longer experience the problem of food shortages.

They have been trained to grow food crops on even very small areas of land.

Some families grow vegetables on their verandahs and balconies, using pots, jerry cans, jars, tins and basins.

The increase in capacity to grow food has reduced the incidence of diseases resulting from poor nutrition.

Few children in the local area now suffer from Kwashiorkor which is a severe form of malnutrition.

The word 'kwashiorkor' comes from the Ga language of coastal Ghana and means 'the disease of the deposed child'.

It is a disease that often affects the older child of a nursing mother who has been pushed aside when a new sibling is born.

Also a greater number of local people now own their own means of transport.

Many years ago Thomas was the only person in Sal who owned a car.

However, today many of the residents are able to buy cars, motorcycles and bicycles.

Sal is now a busy and thriving town.

Residents attribute this growth to Leah and her family.

They hope that Sal town will soon become a city.

Dr. Andy was very happy because all of his dreams had come true.

He had become a doctor, and Thomas` family members became good and honourable.

Andy's best friend, Ethan, became a pilot.

They are both still good friends, and have beautiful girlfriends whom they will be marrying soon.

All in all, being wealthy is good, and being a boss is the best thing ever!

But be mindful of what you say and what you do to others. Who knows? Those you treat well or help today may help you or your family one day.

What you sow is what you reap!

Emilly is also the author of:

The Lost Daughter and The Native Son.

About the author:

Emilly Kembabazi is Ugandan by Nationality.

She was born and raised in the Kanungu district in Southwest Uganda.

She now lives in the outskirts of Kampala, which is the nation's capital city.

Having gained a diploma in journalism and mass communication she uses her skills in storytelling in order to stir her readers imagination.

Emilly's first book - The Lost Daughter and the Native Son was published in 2020.

Through her writing Emilly advocates compassion, love and respect for all, regardless of their race, age, religion or background.

Her conviction is 'Everyone matters'.

Emilly can be contacted by mail:

Kembabazi Emily
P.O. Box 12753
Kampala
Uganda

Email: ek976420@gmail.com

Printed in Great Britain
by Amazon

81554073R10068